Elephant Upstairs

Written by **Patricia Rynearson**

Illustrated by **Jeff Merrill**

I don't like this new place where we
moved. Do you know why?

Because . . . an elephant lives upstairs.

His big feet stomp across the floor.
When they do, our ceiling light sways
and jiggles. I'm afraid the ceiling is
going to break.

I hear him brush his teeth and wash his face.

The gurgling and splashing are horrible.

What if it's a flood?

What if the water comes crashing down on me?

The elephant upstairs is trumpeting.

I think that's how elephants talk.

Dad says maybe he's singing. I don't think so.

Not even an elephant could sing so loudly or so badly.

I hear him run down the apartment stairs.

I hold on to my chair.

When he shuts the door at the bottom of the stairs,

the whole building shakes.

I'm afraid to go to the school bus stop

because I know the elephant will be there.

I don't want to ride in a school bus with an elephant.

"Dad," I say, "I can't go to a school that lets elephants in."

What if the elephant is in my class?
What if I have to share my desk with him?
I'll end up sitting on the floor in my new
dress because there won't be room for
both of us.

When we go to lunch, I'll have to
listen to him crunching and slobbering.
Then I'll feel sick.
I won't be able to eat my sandwich
or my orange or my cookies.

When we go to the playground, he will break
all the swings. The slide will be flat,
and the teeter-totter will only go up . . .
even if the whole class gets on it together.

12

At music, I'll have to hold my ears to keep out
his loud, awful trumpeting. He won't even need
an instrument. He can just use his trunk.
I can't go to school with an elephant
who will ruin my new dress, make me feel sick,
wreck the playground, and trumpet too loud.
"No, Dad," I say, "I'm not going to that school."

But Dad says I have to go anyway.

He holds my hand as we walk to the

bus stop. I peek around him

to see if the elephant is there.

But the only one there is a boy.

His name is Andrew. I can't believe it!

He's the one who lives upstairs,

and he's not an elephant at all!

SCHOOL
BUS
STOP

15